THE BIG SIBLING GETAWAY

Korrie Leer

Albert Whitman & Company
Chicago, Illinois

The boxes came first.

Then the baby.

And then the constant,

WAH! WAH!
WAH! WAH! WAH!

WAH!
WAH!
WAH!
WAH!

WAH!
WAH!
WAH!

nonstop

wailing, sobbing, and whimpering.

WAH!
WAH!
WAH!

WAH!
WAH!
WAH!

Would Cassie's new baby brother
ever stop crying?

She had to get away.

There was one box left.

Cassie still heard crying.
And so...

VROOOOM!

Cassie raced past houses and through forests.

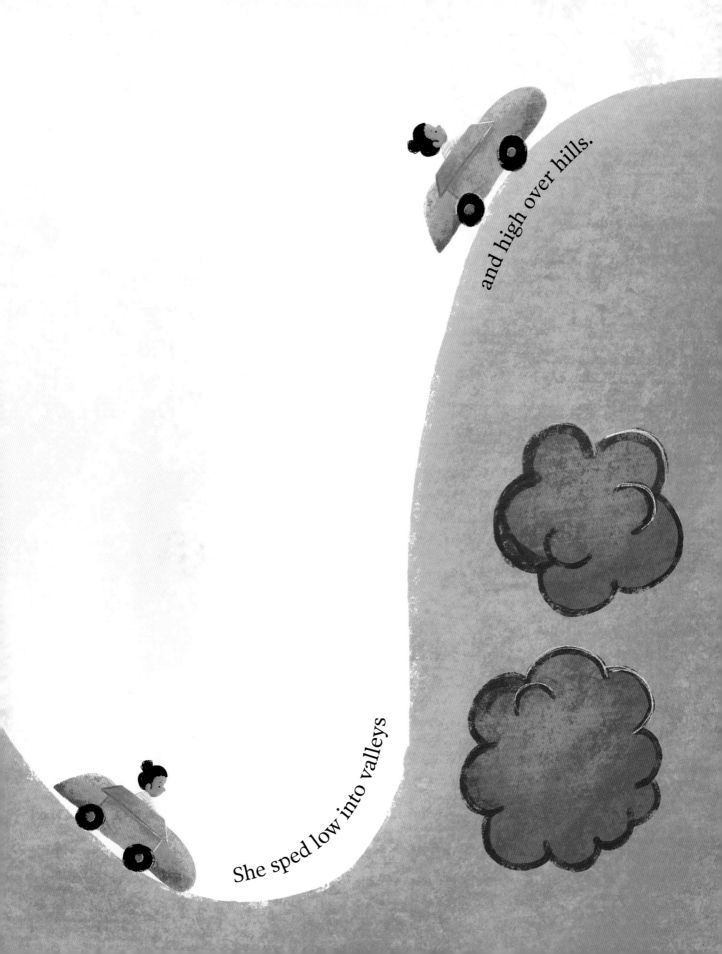

and high over hills.

She sped low into valleys

Cassie drove until she
reached a dead end.

She still heard wailing.
And so...

Cassie cruised past ships and through storms.

Cassie sailed until her boat got beached.

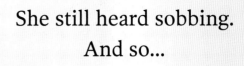

She still heard sobbing.
And so...

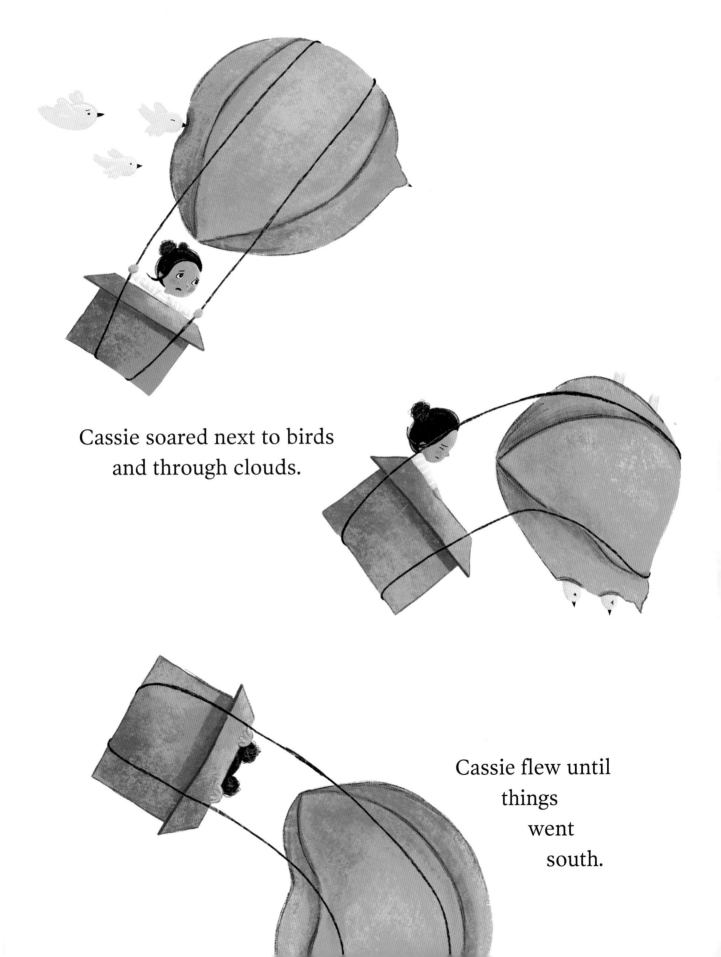

Cassie soared next to birds
and through clouds.

Cassie flew until
things
went
south.

She still heard whimpering.

And so...

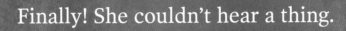

Finally! She couldn't hear a thing.

Peace and quiet at last.

But soon, peace became boring,
and quiet felt lonely.

She couldn't hear a single sniffle, but she was light-years away from everyone she loved.

Even the new baby.

And so...

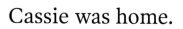

Cassie was home.

Inside, her baby brother
was sleeping.

Outside,
she had the
perfect
escape box

for when he
cried again.

Cassie just wished
she had someone to
bring with her
on her getaways
so she wouldn't
be alone.

And soon enough,

SHE DID.

To Conor and Cassidy, two siblings I'd never try to
get away from . . . anymore—KL

Library of Congress Cataloging-in-Publication
data is on file with the publisher.
Text and illustrations copyright © 2020 by Korrie Leer
First published in the United States of America in 2020
by Albert Whitman & Company
ISBN 978-0-8075-2831-0 (hardcover)
ISBN 978-0-8075-2832-7 (ebook)

Printed in China
10 9 8 7 6 5 4 3 2 1 RRD 24 23 22 21 20

Design by Theresa Venezia

For more information about Albert Whitman & Company,
visit our website at www.albertwhitman.com.